Jade

✳

(**Mary Anne's Big Breakup**)

Lapsley

Other books by Ann M. Martin

P.S. Longer Letter Later
(written with Paula Danziger)
Leo the Magnificat
Rachel Parker, Kindergarten Show-off
Eleven Kids, One Summer
Ma and Pa Dracula
Yours Turly, Shirley
Ten Kids, No Pets
Slam Book
Just a Summer Romance
Missing Since Monday
With You and Without You
Me and Katie (the Pest)
Stage Fright
Inside Out
Bummer Summer

THE KIDS IN MS. COLMAN'S CLASS series
BABY-SITTERS LITTLE SISTER series
THE BABY-SITTERS CLUB mysteries
THE BABY-SITTERS CLUB series
CALIFORNIA DIARIES series

Friends Baby-sitters Club *Forever*

Mary Anne's Big Breakup

Ann M. Martin

AN
APPLE
PAPERBACK

SCHOLASTIC INC.
New York Toronto London Auckland Sydney
Mexico City New Delhi Hong Kong

ISBN 0-590-52326-0

12 11 10 9 8 7 6 5 4 3 2 1   9/9 0 1 2 3 4/0

Printed in the U.S.A.   40

First Scholastic printing, October 1999

The author gratefully acknowledges
Suzanne Weyn
for her help in
preparing this manuscript.

❀ Chapter 1

The postcard I held in my hand should have made me smile. At least a little.

It was pretty funny. And cute.

The card showed a chimp dressed in a frilly, flower-print bathing suit searching through a pile of maps. Above her was the sentence *Without you, I'm lost*.

Only for some reason it didn't make me happy.

I remembered exactly when I'd mailed it to my boyfriend, Logan Bruno. It was when I'd worked as a mother's helper in Sea City, New Jersey. Logan was stuck back here in Stoneybrook, Connecticut, working as a busboy at the Rosebud Cafe.

It was the longest we'd been apart since we first started going out together. I'd sent the card to let him know how much I missed him.

I put the card back in the box and picked up another one, a birthday card.

A photo fluttered out from it. It was a picture of me.

I remembered when my best friend, Kristy Thomas, took the shot. It was the day I'd cut my long brown hair into a chin-length style.

In the picture, my brown eyes looked worried. I had been nervous, hoping Logan would like the haircut.

He did, and he even asked for the picture so he'd have a photo of the new me.

This October afternoon I was sitting in a chair near my bedroom window, looking at that card and at all the other letters, cards, and postcards I'd ever sent to Logan. They were photocopies, actually. Logan had made them for me and given them to me in a shoe box, like the one in which he kept the originals.

I called it *my* bedroom, but somehow I just can't think of the room as mine.

I try to make it feel like home, but it isn't working. I miss my real house so much it hurts. Not just because it was a great old farmhouse (it had been built in 1795). But mostly because it was *my house*.

This house feels so *not* like home that it might as well be a motel.

The reason we're here is that not long ago, our house burned to the ground in a horrible fire.

I still can't believe it happened.

All my life I've heard of people losing everything in fires. I always thought, *How terrible!* But until it happened to me, I had no idea how truly awful the experience is.

I'm not even talking about the fire itself. I mean, that was certainly terrifying. When I think about what might have happened if my kitten, Tigger, hadn't awakened me, I start to shake all over. I still have nightmares about it.

In the dreams I'm standing in my nightgown, outside in the darkness, watching the flames blaze as if they were eating my house.

They aren't particularly imaginative nightmares. That's what really happened.

But, terrible as the fire was, the emotions — sadness, anger, fear — that came after were far worse than the fire itself.

You might say, *Who cares? Stuff can be replaced.*

The only thing is, some stuff can't be replaced. Things like pictures and journals. Scrapbooks. Old invitations. Saved letters. Sentimental things like that.

They matter a lot to me. Partly because, as my friends will tell you, I'm a very sentimental person. And, also, because "stuff" is all I have of my mother, who died when I was a baby.

It's almost as if I've lost her completely now. In fact, it feels as though my past — all thirteen years of it — has suddenly disappeared.

As I sat looking through the box, Sharon knocked on the frame of the open door and stepped in.

Sharon is my stepmom. I'm not exactly sure if I think of Sharon as my mother. (That may be because I don't really know what it feels like to have a mother.) But she's definitely a great person.

She'd pushed her hair back with a velvet headband, and it looked good. "The headband's nice," I said.

Sharon smiled and sat on the end of my bed, across from the chair I was sitting on. "Thanks. It's not too stylish but I'm overdo for a haircut. I forgot to keep the appointment I made the other day. I won't be able to get another one for weeks."

Forgetting an appointment is *so* Sharon. She constantly forgets things, loses things. She misplaces everything she touches.

Sometimes it drives me nuts, because I'm like my father — very organized. I try not to let Sharon's spaciness bother me, though, since she's so terrific in other ways.

"What do you have there?" she asked, nodding toward the box on my lap.

"Everything I've ever written to Logan," I told her.

She frowned, confused. "Why do *you* have them?"

"He loaned them to me so I could re-create my journal. It was his idea. Can you believe he's kept everything I've ever sent him? Isn't that sweet?" I gazed down at the box. "It looks like it's all here."

"That's extremely sweet," Sharon agreed. "Logan is so tenderhearted."

"Definitely," I said.

"I'm glad you found someone who's so much like you."

As I said, I am sentimental. And sensitive. I cry easily.

"Do you think I'm wimpy?" I asked. This question had been on my mind and I needed to talk to someone about it.

"No," Sharon replied, looking surprised. "Why would you ask such a thing?"

I shrugged, not sure how to put it into words.

"Mary Anne, look what you've survived. You've grown up with just your father. I know he's wonderful, but he was very strict. You've handled becoming part of a new family. And I'm so proud of how you've been dealing with things since the fire."

It was nice to hear her say that, because in my mind I was *not* handling the fire well at all. At least I seemed all right to other people.

"What makes you think you're wimpy?" Sharon asked again.

I gazed down at the shoe box on my lap. "I was just looking over all these cards and letters," I said. "The more I read, the more it seemed to me that I never do anything without running it by Logan first. Isn't that wimpy?"

"I don't think so. We all bounce thoughts and ideas off of our friends and families. There's nothing strange in that."

"I was terrified that he wouldn't like my hair when I cut it," I pointed out.

"That was a big change."

"Maybe."

Sharon stood up and checked her watch. "Well, you are definitely not wimpy. Listen, I almost forgot,

I came in to tell you it was five-twenty and it's now five-twenty-five."

"Five-twenty-five!" I cried. "Oh, my gosh!"

I jumped up and the shoe box slid from my lap. Sharon and I grabbed for it at the same time. She caught it first.

"You'd better hurry," she said, handing the box back to me. "I know you don't like to be late for your meetings."

She's right — I don't.

My Baby-sitters Club meeting would begin in five minutes. I'm the secretary, so I need to be on time. Besides, Kristy, our president, hates when anyone is late.

The only good thing about our temporary house is that it's right next door to Claudia Kishi's house. That's where the meetings are held. Even with just five minutes left, I could be on time.

Sharon left, and I set the box down. But as I headed for the door, I noticed a letter on the floor. I scooped it up.

I didn't mean to read it, but the first line caught my eye. I recognized it right away. It was a letter I'd written to Logan when we got back together after the one and only time we'd broken up.

Somehow, I just had to give it a quick look.

Breaking up was the stupidest idea either one of us has ever had, I'd written. *I can't imagine being without you. You're so important to me. I feel like I'm only half a person when I'm not with you.*

Half a person?

Had I really written that?

Had I meant it?

I must have. And it must have felt wonderful and romantic to write it then. But do you know how it felt to read it now? It felt . . . wrong.

Half a person. I certainly didn't feel like half a person without Logan now.

For some reason being part of a couple with Logan didn't feel right. I wasn't sure why. And I wasn't sure what that meant.

But I didn't have time to think about it any longer. If I aimed for some new girls' track record I could still make the meeting on time. I tossed the letter back into the box and raced out the door.

Chapter 2

"Whoa, Mary Anne, who's chasing you?" Kristy asked as I burst breathlessly into Claudia's bedroom. Kristy sat in her usual spot, Claudia's director's chair, her baseball cap pulled down low on her forehead.

I was panting too hard to talk. I think maybe I really had set a new speed record. "What do you mean?" I asked after I caught my breath. "Look at the clock. It's five-thirty. I just made it."

Kristy shrugged. I looked at her hard. This was crazy. Kristy is practically a maniac, a fanatic about being on time.

I gazed around the room. No one but Kristy was there. What was going on? "You don't care if we're on time anymore?"

"Nah. You can come whenever you want."

I stared at her. Kristy is the shortest kid in the

eighth grade. She has shoulder-length brown hair, and brown eyes. She usually wears a sweatshirt, jeans, and sneakers. It's her look. The person in front of me looked like Kristy, but she certainly didn't sound like her.

Suddenly she burst out laughing. "Psych!" she hooted. "Got ya! You should have seen your face!"

"Very funny," I said, smiling. "I thought I'd stepped into the Twilight Zone."

That sent her into another burst of laughter.

"Where is everybody?" I asked.

"Claudia's downstairs getting a snack for Stacey. And in half a minute Stacey's about to be late."

I slid onto Claudia's bed. "That's nice that Claudia's thinking of Stacey," I commented. "Are they friends again?"

Kristy shook her head as her smile faded. "I can't believe they're still fighting. And over a boy too. Of all the dumb things to fight over."

"But Claudia's fixing her a snack," I pointed out. "That's a good sign."

"No, it's not. Claudia told me that since it's part of her club job to provide snacks, she's simply doing her duty."

"Oh," I said glumly. Claudia and our other club member, Stacey McGill, have been best friends ever since Stacey moved to Stoneybrook. Recently, though, they've been fighting over a new guy in school named Jeremy Rudolph.

Since there are only four of us in the club now, it makes things pretty uncomfortable.

Stacey walked in then. She looked sophisticated and pulled together as always. Today she wore a fuzzy aqua sweater, which made her eyes appear even bluer than usual.

It was 5:32.

"Sorry," Stacey said to Kristy. "Jeremy called just as I was walking out the door."

This was not a smart thing to say. To be late for a meeting was bad enough in Kristy's eyes. To be late because you were gabbing with a boy — double trouble.

But before Kristy could say anything to Stacey, Claudia entered with a tray of carrots and celery sticks. Stacey has to eat healthy snacks like that because she has a condition called diabetes. To keep it under control, she has to give herself injections of insulin every day and stick to a strictly scheduled, balanced diet.

"This is for you," Claudia said, practically shoving the tray at Stacey.

"Thank you," Stacey replied icily.

Kristy and I exchanged glances. How long could they keep this up?

Claudia tossed her dark hair behind her shoulders and walked to her bed. She reached under her pillow and pulled out a cellophane bag of potato chips.

None of us thought this was odd. Claudia is crazy about junk food, but her parents aren't. She hides treats all over her room so her parents won't find them. We're used to seeing her retrieve them.

The phone rang and Claudia reached for it. "Hello, Baby-sitters Club," she said. "Hi, Mrs. Rodowsky. . . . Next Saturday at five? Sure. I'll call you right back."

Bending forward, I reached under Claudia's bed and pulled out the club record book. As secretary, I'm in charge of scheduling.

Mrs. Rodowsky is a regular client. We sit for her three boys, Shea, Archie, and Jackie, a lot, so I didn't need Claudia to give me any extra information.

But gazing down at the book, I frowned.

"What's the matter?" Kristy asked.

"No one is free," I informed her. "We're all busy." We keep everyone's schedule listed in the record book so there's never any mix-up assigning a job.

"That's right," Claudia said. "I have a Mural Club meeting that afternoon." Claudia loves art. Although she's not much of a student, she shines when it comes to anything artistic.

She even *looks* artistic. Today she was wearing white painter's coveralls decorated with a wild daisy pattern she'd created herself. Claudia's outfits look great on her, though I don't think I could wear them. But with Claudia's beautiful hair, her sparkling almond-shaped eyes (she's Japanese-American), and her natural grace, it all works.

"You have Mural Club, Kristy is sitting for the Newtons, I'm sitting for the Hills," I explained, "and Stacey is, um, busy."

I knew what she was doing — going bowling with Jeremy. She'd asked me to put it in the record book last week. I didn't want to say this in front of Claudia, though.

It didn't matter. Claudia shot Stacey an angry look anyway.

"We'll have to call Logan," Kristy said.

Logan, in addition to being my boyfriend, used to be an associate member of the BSC. (BSC is what we call the Baby-sitters Club for short.) We used to call him if we had a sitting job no one could handle, like this one. Over the summer, he'd said he wanted to focus on other things, but I was hoping he'd make an exception.

"Logan," I repeated, mixing his name with an unhappy sigh.

Everyone turned and stared at me.

"What?" I asked.

"The way you just said *Logan*," Stacey explained.

"It was the same way a person might say *liver*," Kristy put in.

"Or *homework*," added Claudia.

"So what's the matter?" Kristy asked me.

I sighed again. "It's just that . . ." My voice trailed off. It was so hard to put this into words. "Things don't seem to be . . . the way they were."

"In what way?" Stacey asked.

"I don't know. I used to feel so happy when I knew Logan was coming over or that I'd see him in school. Now I just feel like — *Is he here again?*" I couldn't believe I was saying these things. But they were true.

"Things went flat like that for Josh and me," Claudia said.

"But you and Josh have stayed friends," I replied. "I wonder if Logan and I could."

"Hold on!" Kristy cried, leaning forward in her chair. "What do you mean 'if Logan and I could'? Are you seriously thinking of breaking up with him?"

"Yes," I said. "I think I am."

My friends stared at me as if they couldn't believe what they'd heard.

"I always thought of you and Logan as together forever," said Claud.

"Me too," I replied.

"You two have been through this before," Kristy reminded me. "Remember when we all went to Hawaii and you and Logan tried that TBI thing?"

"Together But Independent," I said. I remembered it very well. It was after Logan and I had broken up and gotten back together. We had been trying to prove to our friends (and maybe to ourselves) that we didn't have to do everything together.

"It made you both miserable," Claudia recalled.

"I know. But things have changed since then."

"I think you're just in some kind of weird mood because of your house," said Kristy.

"You can't exactly blame her for that," Stacey said.

Kristy rolled her eyes. "I'm not blaming her. I'm only trying to say that Mary Anne might be feeling unhappy for other reasons. She's blaming Logan, when maybe it's not Logan who's bothering her at all." But Kristy and I both know this wasn't true. We had talked a lot about Logan over the summer.

"Thank you, Sigmund Freud," I teased.

"Well, Kristy might be right," Claudia said as she dug into the bag of potato chips. "Are you sure Logan is really what's bugging you?"

"Oh, who knows?" I muttered. "He and I are going out together tomorrow. I guess I'll see how I feel then." But I already knew how I felt. I'd known for a long time. I was just too chicken to do anything about it.

While Kristy phoned Logan to see if he could sit for the Rodowskys, I thought about my date with him — and realized I was *not* looking forward to it, even a little.

❋ Chapter 3

Logan was still Logan. It wasn't as if he'd changed in any way. I didn't think that was the problem.

We stood on the corner of Rosedale and Essex Roads in downtown Stoneybrook that Saturday evening. It was only six o'clock. We were still surrounded by dusky light.

I looked up at him. (Logan's taller than I am — most people are — so I'm always looking up.) His face was in shadow. Then a streetlight suddenly snapped on and I saw his face more clearly.

Curly, brownish-blond hair. Same old eyes. He stood with the same easygoing posture as always. He smiled the same. He even sounded the same, with his Kentucky twang. (That was where he lived until his family moved here.)

He hadn't changed much at all since I first met him. So if that were true, what *had* changed?

Me?

Possibly.

"Let's go to the Road Spud," he suggested. That's what he calls the Rosebud Cafe. He picked that up when he worked as a busboy there. All the busboys called it that.

Back then, I'd thought it was so funny. Now, suddenly, it just sounded dumb. Couldn't he think of a new joke? It wasn't as if he still worked there.

"No, not the Rosebud," I said.

"Yeah, come on. Why not? The Spud has good food."

"I don't want to go there, okay?" My words sounded much sharper than I'd meant them to. It was as if I couldn't control my annoyance with him.

"Whoa," he said with a wary laugh. "What's the big deal?"

"The big deal is that I said I didn't want to go but you keep insisting. Don't I get a choice? Do we always have to go where *you* say?"

I'm sure I was taking Logan by surprise. But I couldn't help it. It was how I felt and I couldn't bottle it up inside any longer.

"Of course not. Where would you like to go, Mary Anne?"

"I'm not sure," I admitted.

Logan let out a sigh. "Then would you like me to pick a different place?" he asked.

"No. I want us to pick it together."

As I spoke, I realized that this was exactly the kind of thing that had been bothering me.

Logan was Mr. Take Charge, especially since the fire. He said what we would do. He decided what we liked and didn't like.

I was sick of it.

"How about the Argo Diner?" I suggested.

"Fine," Logan agreed, sounding annoyed.

It bothered me that he was irritated.

Was it so horrible that I made the decision?

Did it bug him that I even *had* an opinion?

We headed down Rosedale toward the Argo. We walked just a bit too fast and didn't look at each other. Anyone watching us could probably tell we were both ticked off.

Logan stopped abruptly in front of a restaurant called Renwick's. "Why don't we go in here?" he suggested. "It's nicer than the Argo."

It was a better place. He was right about that.

But then we'd be going to a place *he'd* picked. Again.

"I chose the Argo," I reminded him.

He nodded toward the Argo, diagonally across the street. "I think it's closed," he said.

"On a Saturday night?" Turning to look, I was surprised to see that the Argo was dark. It *did* appear to be closed. But I wasn't giving in. "Come on," I said, hurrying across the street. "I bet it's open."

Logan was right, though. There was a sign hanging on the door. " 'On vacation until November first,' " Logan read. "I guess we're going to Renwick's."

"Too expensive," I disagreed.

"I have money."

After that, it seemed a little childish to argue. So we went back to Renwick's.

"Remember the first time we came here?" Logan asked, holding the door for me.

How could I forget? We went to Renwick's on our first date. "Of course," I answered snappishly.

"Are you okay?" asked Logan.

"I'm fine," I replied as we entered the restaurant.

A hostess smiled at us, picked up two menus, and led us to a table. The waitress appeared right away, and we ordered.

After she left, we sat and looked at each other. We used to talk a mile a minute whenever we were together. Lately, though, there just didn't seem to be anything to say.

Logan began reading the back of the menu, which told the history of Renwick's restaurant. He didn't seem to know or care that I was just sitting there.

I'd seen couples who acted this way. Older people who'd been married for a thousand years.

Was this what my future with Logan was going to be like? Sitting around together, bored to death?

I remembered when I couldn't wait to see Logan. I told him every single thing that happened to me. It was almost as if nothing were even real until I told it to him.

I remembered it — but I didn't have that feeling anymore.

Now I deliberately didn't share thoughts with him just so they'd stay personal; a part of me that was Mary Anne, alone. Not MaryAnneandLogan, as if we were one person.

Finally, though, I couldn't stand just sitting there another second.

"Logan," I said quietly.

He looked up from the menu. He blinked at me

as if he were returning from some far-off place. Did he really find the history of Renwick's *that* interesting?

Or maybe he was just as bored with me as I had become with him.

You might not believe it, but that thought actually cheered me up.

If he were unhappy, then he wouldn't mind what I was about to say; what, suddenly, I knew I *had* to say.

"Logan," I repeated. "We have to talk."

He straightened in his chair. "I *knew* something was up. What's wrong?"

"It's us," I said. I was afraid I'd lose my nerve if I didn't just come out and say it.

"Us?"

"It's not working out between us these days. You feel it too. Don't you?"

He shook his head slowly.

My throat went dry. He didn't?

"What do you think is the matter?" he asked.

"It's . . . that thing. The problem we've always had," I began.

"What thing?"

"The you-me thing."

"Oh, not that again!" he cried. "I mean, I thought we figured that all out."

"I thought so too, but it's back."

We stared at each other miserably. Anyone listening might not have known what on earth we were talking about, but we knew. When we'd broken up before, it had been because Logan was being too overbearing.

"Well, I'm sorry, Mary Anne," Logan said, breaking the silence. "I'm just being me. I don't ask you to change."

"Yes, you do. You want us to do everything your way. That's asking me to change. And you do it all the time. Plus you're overprotective of me. Like you think I can't do anything on my own."

"You should tell me about it when it happens," he said.

"I do, but you don't hear me."

"You're right, I don't hear you. Because I don't think you speak up. Only you think you do."

I wasn't quite sure how to answer that. And just then our food arrived.

It was horrible. I mean, the food was fine. But eating it was miserable. I felt as if I were swallowing lumps of clay that kept sticking in my throat.

As I choked down my food, I thought about what Logan had said. Was it true that I never spoke up?

Maybe there was a little fault on both sides. It might be that I didn't let my feelings be known enough. Even if that was true, it was also true that Logan didn't listen enough.

He was always so sure his way was the best way.

I couldn't put up with it any longer.

Logan put down his hamburger. "So what do you want to do?" he asked, his voice a little angry. "Break up?"

Part of me couldn't believe I was doing it, but I nodded.

The color drained from his face.

"Yes," I said in a small, dry voice.

❋ Chapter 4

It was awful! Logan couldn't have looked any more surprised and horrified if I'd cracked the plate over his head.

I realized then that when he had asked, "Do you want to break up?" he was being sarcastic.

He'd expected me to say, "Of course not."

Tears jumped into my eyes. Under the table, I dug the fingernails of my right hand into my left palm.

I did it to hold back the tears.

If I started crying, I knew I'd take back my words. I'd say I didn't really want to break up, that I was just in a bad mood — anything to make Logan feel better again.

And that wasn't what I needed to do.

The waitress passed near our table. "Check, please," Logan said. She nodded.

Logan turned back to me and seemed about to speak. Then he laughed bitterly. "I did it again," he said.

"What?" I asked.

"I asked for the check without asking if you wanted to leave."

He was right. He *had* done it again.

It didn't seem the right time to make a big deal out of it, though.

"It's okay," I told him. "I'm not very hungry anymore either."

"See? That's just it, Mary Anne," he said. "I know you so well. I know what you'll like and won't like. So I just go ahead and act on that. Is that so bad?"

"You *don't* always know," I said quietly. "You're just always so sure that you do. Only sometimes you're wrong."

"But a lot of times I'm right."

The waitress put the check on the table. We pooled our money and left it there.

Without talking, we left the restaurant. Logan walked ahead of me. By the time I came through the front door, he was already standing on the corner with his back to me. I took a deep breath and looked up at him. "Logan, I —"

I cut myself short.

Logan was crying.

The sight of his crumpled, red-eyed face stopped me cold. How could I do this to him?

Images flooded into my mind. I remembered all the fun we'd had together, all the times Logan had been there for me. I wished — wished really hard — that I could find my way back to the way it had been, that I could feel the same way about Logan now as I'd felt then.

I couldn't, though.

"Are you sure this is what you want?" Logan asked, wiping his eyes with a quick, rough movement.

"Yes," I forced myself to say.

"Okay, then," he said, looking away from me. "Let's go home."

Anyone else might have stomped off and left me to go home by myself. But not Logan. It was one of the things I'd always loved about him.

"Come on," he said.

I knew he'd insist on walking me home, even if every step of the way was miserable for him. So I didn't even bother to argue. I just fell into step alongside him as we headed toward my house.

We didn't speak for almost four blocks.

Then I couldn't stand the silence any longer.

"Logan, I really want us to stay friends," I said.

He mumbled a reply, but his voice was so low I couldn't make out the words. "What?" I asked.

"I said, 'I don't think so,' " he told me, nearly shouting this time.

"Why?"

"Because that never works."

"It can." I was walking fast now, trying to keep up with Logan's unusually fast pace. "Stacey is friends with Robert, and I think she still talks to Ethan. Claudia is friendly with Josh."

"That's great for them," Logan snapped. "But it won't work for us."

I grabbed his elbow, forcing him to slow down. "Why can't we be friends?" I pleaded.

"Mary Anne," he said angrily, "if you want to be my friend so much, why are you doing this?"

"Because being friends is different than being boyfriend and girlfriend."

He began walking again, even faster than before. I was nearly jogging to keep up with him. By the time we reached my house, I was almost breathless.

I expected Logan to stop. He didn't even slow down, though.

Without turning toward me, he just lifted his

hand to wave. " 'Bye, Mary Anne," he said, and kept going.

I stood on the sidewalk, watching him.

Now that he was gone, I could cry.

My tears overflowed, running down my face. All of a sudden I didn't know if I'd done the right thing or the stupidest thing possible.

I'm not sure how long I stood there. It might have been one minute or five. But, after awhile, I felt a gentle hand on my shoulder.

Wiping my eyes, I realized Claudia was standing beside me.

"Mary Anne, what's wrong?" she asked. Even in the darkness I could see that her face was full of worry.

"I just broke up with Logan," I told her in a choked voice.

Her hand flew to her mouth. "I didn't think you'd really do it," she confessed. "I thought you were just letting off steam yesterday."

I shook my head.

"How did he take it?"

"He's pretty upset."

My tears began flowing again. I put my hand over my face, but I couldn't stop them.

Claudia put her arm around my shoulders.

"Wow, it's a good thing I was on my way home. Otherwise you'd be out here all by yourself."

I wanted to tell her it was all right, that she didn't have to stand outside with me. When I started to speak, though, all that came out was this awful-sounding choked sob.

With her arm still around me, Claudia began moving us both along. "Come on," she said. "Come to my house and we can talk."

Chapter 5

"Pringles or Cracker Jacks?" Claudia asked, taking one of each from her bottom dresser drawer.

"Some of both, please," I said. I sat on her bed, my chin propped in my hands. I wasn't sure that junk food would make me feel any better, but it wouldn't hurt.

"You're right," Claudia said as she opened the box of Cracker Jacks. "This is definitely a two-treat night."

I smiled. A little. At least I'd stopped crying. Although I was now a puffy wreck and couldn't keep from sniffing.

Claudia handed me the Cracker Jacks. "Do you think you guys can be friends?" she asked as she dug into the Pringles.

"I suggested it, but the idea seemed to make Logan even more upset."

She nodded thoughtfully. "He probably doesn't think you mean it."

"But I do. After all we've shared, how could we just not be anything to each other?"

"I understand how you feel. But being friends with a guy after you break up with him is hard. Maybe impossible."

"But you're friends with Josh," I reminded her.

She shifted uneasily in her chair. "Well, yes and no."

"What do you mean?"

"We're not enemies. We stop to say hi, and we talk a little, but I'm not sure I'd say we're friends. Not the way you and I are friends, or the way I'm friends with Kristy or Abby or the way I used to be friends with you-know-who."

"Why don't you and Stacey make up?" I asked.

"I don't want to talk about that right now."

"Okay."

"What I mean about remaining friends," Claudia continued, "is that not being mad at each other is *not* the same as being friends. Josh and I thought we'd still be able to hang out and do things together, but it hasn't worked out that way. And we were friends *be-fore* we started going out. You'd think we could go back to that. But, somehow . . . I don't know. Maybe it will be different for you and Logan."

"I don't know how it can be," I said, "if Logan doesn't even want to try." My voice broke and the tears came back. The next thing I knew I was crying all over my Cracker Jacks.

Janine, Claudia's sixteen-year-old sister, poked her head into the room. "Claudia, I can't find — " She broke off when she saw my face. "Mary Anne, are you okay?" she asked.

Janine is an actual genius with a sky-high IQ. Sometimes she talks and acts like a college professor or something. But she's definitely human. And she broke up with her boyfriend, Jerry, not long ago.

"Mary Anne just dumped her boyfriend," Claudia told her.

"Oh, no. Logan? That's terrible. But if it had to be done, you'll be glad you've done it, later."

I spoke through my tears. "You're right, I guess. But I'm not happy about it now."

Standing up, I rubbed my eyes. I wasn't ready to talk about this in any logical way. "I'm sorry, but I think I should go. I'm rotten company right now."

"No, please," Janine protested as I grabbed my jacket from Claudia's director's chair and brushed past her.

Claudia bolted out into the hall after me. "Don't go. You need to be around friends right now."

"I'll be okay."

"I'll call you later," Claudia said as I headed down the stairs.

When I got home, the house was still dark except for the lamp Sharon and my dad leave lit in the front hall. They'd said earlier that they might go to the movies, and I guessed that they had.

No one home. Good, I thought as I let myself in the front door. I just wanted to go to my room and cry until I fell asleep.

I was halfway up the stairs when the phone began ringing. I froze. Maybe it was Logan.

Hurrying back down, I grabbed the phone on the third ring, just before the answering machine picked up. "Hello?"

"Hi, Mary Anne, it's me." It was my stepsister, Dawn, calling from California.

"Oh, hi," I said. With the cordless phone to my ear, I wandered into the living room and sat down on the couch.

"Hey, you sound shaky. What's the matter?" she

asked. Dawn and I were friends before her mom married my dad and we became stepsisters. (In fact, it was our idea to get them back together, since they'd dated as teenagers.)

"I just broke up with Logan," I told her. This was the second time I'd said this and it wasn't getting any easier.

"Wow! Again?"

"This time it's for good."

"Are you sure? You two have been through this before."

"I'm positive," I said. "It's the same old problem. It just keeps coming back and I can't take it anymore."

"Logan's crowding you?" she said thoughtfully. She was silent for a moment. "Then you did the right thing."

"You think so?"

"Definitely. Logan's a great guy, but he does *not* need to be in charge all the time."

"But sometimes that's what I liked about him," I admitted.

"Yeah, but you're changing. You're more your own person now, and I can see how he could get on your nerves."

"Really?"

"Absolutely. You've changed since I first met you — in good ways. You even look different."

I supposed what she said was true. When I first met Dawn — and Logan — I was still wearing my hair in braids. My dad was very strict about how I dressed, and as a result, I looked a lot more childish than my friends did. I probably acted younger too. But around that time, I started asking for more independence. And after Dad married Sharon, she encouraged him to lighten up on me too.

The front doorknob rattled. Dad and Sharon had returned. "Hi, Dawn's on the phone," I told them.

Sharon's face lit up. I know she misses Dawn a lot and still doesn't completely understand why Dawn (and her younger brother, Jeff) chose to live with their father and his new wife in California, instead of here with us. I don't understand it either, but I guess I accept it more easily than Sharon does.

"Oh, let me talk to her," Sharon said.

"I'm putting your mom on," I told Dawn.

"Okay, 'bye. You did the right thing, Mary Anne."

"Thanks. I hope so," I replied glumly.

I handed Sharon the phone and headed upstairs. I was in my room barely half a minute when Dad appeared and stood in my doorway. "What's the matter?" he asked.

"Is it that obvious?"

He nodded.

"I broke up with Logan," I told him.

He came into the room and sat on my desk chair. "I'm not surprised."

His not being surprised surprised me. "Why not?" I asked.

"I thought I noticed a certain lack of enthusiasm lately when Logan was around."

I was impressed. I didn't think Dad was that observant. And I didn't even know I'd been acting unenthusiastic.

"Logan's great," I said. "But he's just . . . I don't know . . . too much."

"I suppose you did what you thought was best," he said. "But if that's true, then why are you so upset?"

"Because I've really hurt him."

"Someone always gets hurt in a breakup," said Dad. "But he'll get over it."

"I guess I'm disappointed too," I added. "Deep

down, I always thought Logan and I would be like Sharon and you."

Dad smiled. "It wasn't all that smooth," he reminded me. I knew the story. Sharon's parents had thought Dad wasn't good enough for Sharon, so they sent her off to college in California just to separate her from him. That's where she met and married Dawn's father and had Dawn and Jeff. But then they divorced, and Sharon and the kids returned to Stoneybrook — where Dawn and I learned about our parents' past. (We were looking through Sharon's high school yearbook.) We arranged for my dad and Sharon to meet again. And the rest is romantic history.

"Maybe things will work out for you and Logan in the end," Dad suggested, "just as they did for Sharon and me."

"I don't think so. I don't think Logan can change that much."

Dad stood up. "Who knows? Life is funny." He kissed me on the top of my head. "Good night, honey. Try not to think about it anymore tonight. Get some rest."

"Thanks, Dad," I said as he walked out.

I stretched out on my bed and closed my eyes. I didn't really plan to sleep, just rest. My eyes stung from crying and it felt good to shut them.

Outside my room, I heard the phone ring. Sitting up, I wondered if it was Logan.

"Mary Anne," Sharon called from the stairs. "Phone!"

My heart pounded. It would be hard to face another conversation with him. My shoulders tightened. No matter how upset he was, I couldn't change my mind.

I dragged myself off the bed and met Sharon in the stairway. She handed me the cordless phone. "It's Kristy."

My body slumped with relief as I took the phone. "Hi."

"Mary Anne! What happened? I talked to Claudia, so I know a little. But what happened? I can't believe you really broke up with him."

I drew in a deep breath. The news had already spread. I realized at that moment that it was going to keep spreading — first to the rest of my friends, and then all through the eighth grade, and all through school.

Everyone knows Logan. He's such a good athlete. And everyone knows I'm his girlfriend, or *was* his girlfriend.

"You knew I was thinking about it," I reminded Kristy.

"Yeah, but how did it happen?"

I sat on the steps and told her. I knew I'd be telling the story a lot over the next week or so, so I had to get used to it.

As I spoke, though, I began to wonder again if I really *had* done the right thing.

�֍ Chapter 6

On Sunday I just hid away from the world. My friends all called, offering to come over. I thanked them but said no. I had homework to do, and it seemed easier to think about that than talking about Logan all day.

But on Monday, I couldn't hide any longer. There was no way to avoid school.

I didn't really want to avoid it, anyway. Most of the time, I like being at school.

It was Logan I hoped to avoid, although I knew it would be practically impossible.

That morning, Stoneybrook Middle School (we call it SMS, for short) seemed different to me. I stopped to look at it, to see if the walls had been painted over the weekend, the floors had been changed, or if something else had been done to make it appear so different. Nothing had been changed, though.

The kids seemed different too.

It's hard to describe what I sensed. Usually I head down the hall to my locker without thinking anything of it. I smile and wave to kids along the way. Everything's fine.

This day, though, I had the feeling that kids stopped talking when I passed. The guys and girls I usually nod and wave to shot me these sickly, sympathetic smiles.

Some of Logan's teammates turned toward their lockers as I passed.

Was it a coincidence, or were they intentionally avoiding me?

A couple of guys shot me angry glances. At least I thought they did. Was it my imagination?

Kristy was waiting at my locker when I arrived there. "How's it going?" she asked.

"I don't know." I leaned against the locker. "I feel weird. Does everyone in the whole school already know about Logan and me, or am I being paranoid?"

Kristy hesitated.

"Everyone knows, don't they?" I said.

She nodded. "Sort of."

"Well, what's the big deal? I haven't committed a crime. It's not anyone else's business anyway."

"You're totally right," Kristy agreed.

"I know I am," I muttered, putting my books into my locker. I was thinking about which books to bring with me when Kristy poked my arm sharply.

Startled, I dropped a book. "That hurt!" I said.

"Sorry," Kristy murmured. "I just wanted to alert you."

I followed her intense gaze down the hall and instantly saw the problem.

Logan was approaching — flanked by a couple of his friends from the track team.

He stopped beside my locker. "Hello, Mary Anne," he said stiffly.

"Hello," I replied, trying to make my voice as natural as possible.

His friends glowered at me.

Logan was wearing an injured expression, a look that said he was a poor, suffering soul.

A horrible silence followed. Then Logan continued down the hall, followed by his pals.

I slumped against my locker, feeling as if I'd been drained of all my energy.

"Don't let him get to you," Kristy said angrily.

"I won't. But it's kind of upsetting to think that

now the entire track team probably hates me."

"And the baseball and football teams too," Kristy added.

"Kristy! Was that supposed to make me feel better?"

"I'm sorry. Anyway, you know they don't *hate* you. Face it," she added, "guys stick together. Especially guys on teams. And Logan is on three teams."

"Why does he have to be so athletic?" I muttered. "You know what else bothers me? That Logan has to surround himself with all his friends. Does he think he needs protection from me?"

"Maybe it wasn't his idea," Kristy offered.

She had a point.

"But still," I argued. "That only means *his friends* think he needs protection from me. And did you hear the way he said hello?" I imitated his stiff, suffering voice. " 'Hel-*looo*, Mary Anne.' "

"It *was* pretty stupid," Kristy agreed.

I slammed my locker shut. "Logan's acting so wounded and noble. He's trying to make it seem like I'm some big villain, as if I deliberately did something to hurt him just for the fun of it. He acts as if this isn't hurting me as much as it's hurting him."

"I've never seen you so angry," Kristy said as we began walking down the hall.

"Do you blame me?" I asked. " 'Hello, Mary Anne,' " I mimicked his voice again.

"I can see how it would bug you," Kristy said, "but he's upset. He can't help it if his friends are jerks. Give him a break."

"Give *him* a break?" I cried. "Whose friend are you anyway?"

"I thought you and Logan were both my friends."

I stared at her, surprised by her answer.

I'd expected her to say that of course she was *my* friend. But her answer had been honest. She was friends with both of us.

"That's true," I mumbled. "You can do what you like."

"Don't be mad about it," Kristy said.

"I'm not mad," I told her, which was mostly true. I wasn't deep down, really mad. I was more upset, and I wanted to know I had at least one true-blue best friend by my side — Kristy. "Sorry I snapped at you. It's just that everything feels so weird right now."

For the rest of that morning I did a pretty good job of not thinking about Logan. I accomplished that by paying total attention to my teachers.

I didn't really think about him until I was in the

hallway outside the cafeteria. I knew he'd be in the lunchroom. How would I handle it? What would *he* do? The closer I came to the door, the tighter the knot in my stomach grew.

As I approached, I saw Stacey talking to Jeremy. They were laughing together, and seemed so happy. Logan and I had been like that. Why couldn't things have stayed that way?

Stacey noticed me and said good-bye to Jeremy. "How *are* you?" she asked, hurrying to my side.

"Okay." (I may not have had a whole team to surround me, but I felt grateful for my friends.)

Stacey leaned close and lowered her voice. "Logan is already in the lunchroom. He's surrounded by most of the baseball team."

"It was the track team this morning," I told her.

"What are they protecting him from?" she asked. "You?"

"I suppose."

"Well, you're pretty tough and scary, Mary Anne. I can see why he needs protecting." She laughed. "Boys!" she said, as if that explained everything.

We walked into the cafeteria together. My friends were already seated at our usual table. Stacey and I joined the lunch line.

As I waited, my eyes traveled to the table where Logan sits with his pals on days when he doesn't eat lunch with my friends and me. He wasn't there.

I scanned the cafeteria, looking for Logan, and spotted him ahead of us in the line.

He stared out sadly into the cafeteria. I guessed that he was trying to find me, just as I'd been searching for him a moment before.

Another person would probably have thought he seemed okay. But I could see something in his eyes that made me shiver.

He reminded me of a little boy lost in a department store, in that moment he first realizes his mom or dad is gone — just before he starts to cry.

I wanted to put my arms around him. Tell him everything was going to be all right, and that we could be friends and I'd always be there to help if he needed me.

I knew it wouldn't be the right thing to do, though.

And then, for the first time since Saturday night, an icy-cold feeling of loneliness crept through me.

Logan was really not a part of my life anymore.

I don't think I'd realized it until that moment.

❋ Chapter 7

That afternoon, at our BSC meeting, I opened the record book and gasped. "Oh, no! I'm supposed to sit at Logan's house tomorrow. Mrs. Bruno booked the job over three weeks ago."

"Why isn't Logan watching Kerry and Hunter?" Kristy asked.

"Football practice has started."

"Then that means he won't be there," Claudia pointed out.

That made me feel calmer. "You're right," I said. "Still . . . it's going to be weird."

"I'm sitting for Charlotte Johanssen tomorrow," Stacey said. "I could bring her over to the Brunos' house and do two jobs at once if you like."

"Or I can leave Mural Club a little early and cover for you," Claudia volunteered.

"I wanted to study for a test, but I could squeeze the job in," Kristy added.

"Thanks, you guys," I said. "But I really should go. The Brunos have been like a second family to me. I don't want them to think I don't care about them anymore. Kerry and Hunter are such great kids."

Kerry is Logan's ten-year-old sister and Hunter is his five-year-old brother. I've been very close to them. I hoped that wouldn't change.

"No, I definitely have to go," I said firmly. "Just keep your fingers crossed that Mrs. Bruno gets home before football practice lets out, and everything will be fine."

My friends held up three sets of crossed fingers.

Even though I was sure I'd made the right decision, I felt anxious about the sitting job all day Tuesday.

That morning, I saw Logan in the hall. He was alone.

"Hi," he said.

"Hi," I replied. We stood there, neither of us knowing what to say.

" 'Bye," I finally blurted out as I hurried off.

Even though it was an awkward moment, it left me feeling slightly better. Maybe things would improve a little each day. It was an encouraging thought.

After school, I headed to the Brunos' house. They live on Burnt Hill Road, where my old house used to be. To get there I had to pass the burned-out remains.

Nothing much was left but a big hole in the ground where the basement had been and the barn we were now converting into our new house. The hole was almost filled with charred wood, which lay in a black heap. The melted shell of the microwave sat inside the blackened, peeling bathtub. The oven, refrigerator, washing machine, dryer, and dishwasher were also sooty, blistered, and warped but still there. Anything that was still usable had been taken away. There hadn't been much.

I wondered which heap of ashy cinders had been my bed, which ashes were once my photo albums, my books, my CDs.

It amazed me that after all this time I could still smell smoke. More than the sight, the smell brought back the horrible memory.

An odd idea popped into my head. Had my entire world changed on the night of the fire? In a way, it seemed so. Not on the outside but maybe inside.

The thought made me uncomfortable and I pushed it out of my mind.

Turning up my jacket collar against the cold, I hurried on. I couldn't stand to see my house in its ruined state.

When I arrived at the Brunos', Logan's mom answered the door. "Hi, Mary Anne, come on in."

Her behavior was so friendly and normal I wondered if she even knew about Logan's and my breakup. She was hurrying off to a meeting about setting up a book fair at Kerry's school.

"Where are the kids?" I asked. They usually run out to greet me, but today they were nowhere in sight.

Mrs. Bruno pulled on her jacket and checked around. "Gee, I don't know. They were here a minute ago. Kerry! Hunter!"

They still didn't appear.

Mrs. Bruno walked to the stairs and called up to them. "Kids!"

Hunter came down the stairs. He peered at me through the railings, frowning. Mrs. Bruno might not know something was going on, but I could see that Hunter did.

"What's the matter?" Mrs. Bruno asked. "Mary Anne is here!"

Kerry stood on the stairs behind Hunter and put her hand on his slim shoulder. "Hello, Mary Anne," she said.

I couldn't believe it! She sounded *exactly* the way Logan had on Monday. Hurt and noble and angry at the same time.

She was definitely aware of the breakup.

And definitely mad at me.

Mrs. Bruno frowned at Hunter and Kerry, confused. Then, turning her wrist, she glanced at her watch. "I'd better go."

"We'll be fine," I assured her.

"Okay," she replied with one more perplexed glance at her kids. "All right, Mary Anne, I'll be at the elementary school. The numbers there are posted on the fridge, and so is my cell phone number. I'll be back around six."

Six! I thought, panicked. Logan's football practice wouldn't last until six.

"Don't bother about dinner," she continued, grabbing her purse from a doorknob. "I'll cook for these guys when I get home. Mr. Bruno's working late and Logan's stopping off for pizza with some of the guys, so I won't have to worry about them."

Logan was stopping for pizza. Good. I calmed down. That would probably keep him out later than six. I was safe.

I closed the door behind Mrs. Bruno and turned

to find Kerry and Hunter facing me, arms folded, their expressions set angrily into scowls.

"I guess we should talk," I said.

"You dumped Logan!" Kerry cried. "Are you crazy? How could you do that?"

"Yeah!" Hunter shouted.

"We definitely have to talk," I said. "Can we please go sit in the living room?"

Still scowling at me, Hunter and Kerry moved to the living room.

"If Logan's not good enough for you anymore, then I suppose we're not either," Kerry said as she threw herself onto the couch. Hunter hurled himself onto the cushions beside her.

I sat at the edge of the easy chair across from them. "Kerry, that's not what's going on," I began. "I don't think I'm too good for Logan."

"Then why did you break up with him?"

"Because it just wasn't . . . working," I replied.

Kerry frowned. "That makes *no* sense."

"Think of it like this. Did you ever have a friend in one grade who you weren't such good friends with in the next grade?"

"I'm not even in a grade!" Hunter cried.

"Kindergarten is a grade," I told him. "It's true,

though. You probably don't know what I mean. But I bet Kerry does."

Kerry nodded. "I still don't see what it has to do with Logan, though."

"Well, there are some kids who you have a lot in common with in . . . say . . . the third grade, but by fourth grade you don't have as much in common. You've both changed. So you find different friends."

"Does this mean you found a new boyfriend?" Kerry asked.

"No! It means Logan and I have changed. We don't always like the same things as much as we used to. It happens."

Judging from Kerry's unmelting frown, I still wasn't making sense to her. But hearing my own words was helping me to understand the reasons I'd done what I'd done. At least I was getting through to me.

"I get it!" Hunter exclaimed. "I used to like this kid named Tyler but now I think he's a big bully. Yesterday he hit my friend. Now I hate him."

"It's sort of like that," I agreed. "Only Logan didn't do anything bad to me, and I don't hate him."

"But you don't like him either," Kerry added.

"I *do* like him," I insisted. "I just don't think he and I should be boyfriend and girlfriend anymore."

"I don't know. . . ." Kerry's face had softened a little.

"Try to believe me," I pressed on. "I like Logan, and I still like the two of you. I hope we can always be friends."

"Sure!" Hunter said.

"I guess so," Kerry agreed less enthusiastically.

"Great," I said. "Now, what would you two like to do?"

Hunter had a new computer game he wanted to show me. "That's so babyish," Kerry said, but sat down at the computer desk to play with us anyway.

The game was cute and it made the time pass quickly. Still, when I heard the front door open, I knew it couldn't be six o'clock yet.

My heart raced. It could only be one person.

"Logan!" Hunter cried, jumping up from the chair and running to his big brother. "Good news. Mary Anne told us she still likes you!"

Logan looked at me quickly, his face full of surprise.

At that moment, I wished I could disappear.

"Mary Anne?" he said to me quietly.

I stood up and faced him. "Of course I like you. I'll always like you."

His face lit up hopefully. "Then maybe we can work this out?"

My stomach twisted into a knot. My mouth went dry. Flinging open the coat closet, I clutched my jacket, yanking it off the hanger. "I don't think so, Logan. Look, I have to go. You can watch the kids now."

" 'Bye," I called to the kids as I hurried outside.

With my head down, I began to run toward my house. I needed to go into my room, shut the door, and speak to no one.

❁ Chapter 8

The next day in school Kristy and I passed one of Logan's track team friends, a guy named Lew Greenberg. I said hi to him and he looked right through me.

"What's with him?" I asked.

"I guess he thinks he's being loyal to Logan."

"I'm his friend too! At least I thought so."

"Some kids feel as if they have to take sides when stuff like this happens," said Kristy.

"Guys sure do," I agreed.

"They'll get over it," Kristy said with a shrug.

I saw Jim Poirier trotting down the hall toward us. He was on the football team with Logan.

"Hi, Jim," I said.

"Oh. Mary Anne," he mumbled, pretending he

hadn't seen me until that second. Then he hurried away.

"Did you see that?" I cried.

Kristy shook her head in disgust. "Who cares about Jim Poirier? He's a dope anyway."

"I just can't believe this," I said.

As we stood there, a guy named Dave Griffin approached me.

"What does he want?" I whispered to Kristy. "I hope he's not delivering some hate letter signed by all the boys in the school."

Kristy nudged me with her elbow, as if to say, *Don't talk crazy.* But I noticed she stared at him suspiciously, folding her arms.

"Hi," he said to both of us.

"Hi," Kristy and I replied together.

There was an awkward silence. Dave kept looking at me. His expression was friendly, not angry or threatening in any way. That made me relax and stop worrying that he was a messenger from the We-Hate-Mary-Anne-Because-She-Dumped-Logan Club.

"I have to go," Kristy said suddenly. Before I could say anything, she was hurrying down the hall.

What was going on?

"Mary Anne," Dave said, "I heard about you and Logan."

I tensed up again.

"So I was wondering if you're going to the Fall Fling."

"What?" I asked.

"The dance?"

"Oh, right," I said. I sort of knew it was coming up but I hadn't paid much attention to it. Logan and I usually decided at the last minute whether we wanted to go to things like that.

"So?" Dave asked.

"So what?" I replied. "Oh, the dance. No, I don't think I'll be going. Why? Did you want me to work on some committee or something?"

"No. I was asking if you'd like to go to the dance with me."

I felt so dumb!

I hadn't even realized.

"Me?" I gasped. It had been so long since a boy had asked me out.

"Would you like to go?" he asked again.

"Oh . . . um," I stammered.

A confused expression came over Dave's face. "Did I hear the story wrong?" he asked. "You did break up with Logan, didn't you?"

"Yes, we broke up. I just don't think I'm ready to go out on a date yet. I'm not . . . ready."

"Are you sure?"

"No," I admitted. But then, I didn't want to mislead him. "I mean yes. I'm sure."

"Okay," Dave replied. "If you change your mind, give me a call. When you look up our number in the phone book, look under Dave. That's my dad's name too."

"All right," I agreed. "And thanks for the invitation."

"No problem," he answered, giving me a wave as he left.

What a nice guy, I thought, watching him go. Because of Logan, I hadn't paid much attention to other boys at SMS. At least not in a romantic way.

I barely knew Dave. It surprised me that he'd asked me out. Had he liked me all along but never asked me out because everyone knew I was Logan's girlfriend?

I was so involved with my thoughts that I didn't notice Logan coming down the hall until he was only a few feet away from me. "Hi, Mary Anne."

I jumped a little. "Hi, Logan."

"You know, you didn't have to run out of the house the way you did yesterday."

I could feel my face heating up and knew I was

blushing with embarrassment. "This is all so confusing," I said.

It was the wrong thing to say.

"You mean, you're not sure about it?" A hopeful look came into his eyes.

"No, that's not what I meant," I said quickly. "I mean I still want to be your friend, but it seems like we're at war. And I don't understand why that's happening."

"Oh." He looked away from me. "You want this to be easy, but breaking up is never easy. I guess that's just how it is."

"I'm sorry, Logan," I said quietly. "I'm sorry I've hurt you."

"Whatever," he said with a shrug. Then he walked away.

It was a depressing conversation, and pretty much wrecked my mood for the rest of the morning.

Lunchtime wasn't any better.

From the table where I sat with my friends, I couldn't stop myself from sneaking peeks at Logan. He was sitting with the other guys, but he wasn't his usual happy self.

It made me miserable to think that I was the cause of his unhappiness. I was so used to thinking of

Logan's happiness as well as my own. Now, here I was, the one who had hurt him.

After dismissal, Claudia met me at my locker. She doesn't usually do that. She used to meet Stacey. But since they've been fighting, that's changed.

"How did things go with Logan today?" she asked as I packed up my books.

"Terrible. I know he wants us to get back together. And, in a lot of ways, that would be the easiest thing to do. But it wouldn't be the *right* thing, at least not for me. I miss him, though. I feel so weird."

Claudia sighed. "Everything is so complicated."

"Tell me about it," I replied.

We began walking down the hall together. We passed Jeremy and Stacey standing at Jeremy's locker. I waved. Claudia pretended she didn't notice them.

"She makes me so mad," Claudia grumbled once we were far enough away.

"Can't you just forget about it?"

"I wish I could, but I think about Jeremy all the time. I'm positive he would have liked me if she hadn't jumped in between us. I can't believe she was ever my best friend."

I nodded, remembering when I thought of Logan as one of my best friends. There was also a time when I'd thought of my stepsister, Dawn, as a best friend. Then she'd moved away.

Why did things have to change?

"At least you and I aren't pretending," Claudia said.

"What do you mean?"

"I could pretend I wasn't angry with Stacey," she explained. "And you could act like you were still perfectly happy with Logan."

We left the building and cut across the school yard. It was a breezy day, and the wind tossed our hair around our faces as we walked.

What Claudia said was true. We'd created the situations we were in.

Why?

We'd wanted to be honest, I suppose. We didn't want to fake emotions we didn't feel. That, at least, had to be a good thing.

"It takes guts to say how you really feel," Claudia continued, "especially when it's going to make someone unhappy."

"That's true. It does take guts. Everything was so much easier as a couple. I can already see that it's going to be harder on my own. Much harder."

"You'll be okay, though," Claud said. The confidence in her voice made me feel braver. She sounded so sure. Maybe she was right.

I smiled. "It might be interesting to discover who I am without Logan. Exciting, even."

Mary Anne Spier, single girl, I thought. What would that girl be like?

I couldn't imagine.

❀ Chapter 9

"Mary Anne, I had the greatest idea," Stacey said to me in the hall the next day just before lunch. "I can't believe I didn't think of it before."

"What?" I asked.

"Pete Black."

"What about him?"

"We'll get Pete Black to take you to the Fall Fling!" She smiled proudly, as if she'd said something unbelievably brilliant that was about to make us both millionaires.

Her smile slowly faded. Probably because I wasn't smiling back at her.

"What's wrong with Pete?" she asked. "He's a great guy. I got to know him much better when we worked together on that video project for the movie-making class. And he's cute, don't you think?"

"Pete's nice," I agreed.

"Good," Stacey said. "I already asked if he's taking someone to the dance and he's not. And listen to this." She paused dramatically. "When we were talking yesterday, he asked me, 'Did Mary Anne dump Logan for another guy?' "

Her big blue eyes went wide with excitement. I had a feeling she expected me to jump up and down.

"He's nosy like everyone else," I said.

"He's not nosy, he's *interested*. Interested in you. Why else would he have asked the question?"

"I told you, he's nosy."

"There's more," she said eagerly. Stacey moved closer to me and lowered her voice. "Emily Bernstein told me that Pete said to her — wait till you hear this — 'Mary Anne won't be single for long.' He thinks you're really pretty and nice."

"Wow, he said that?" I'd had no idea Pete thought I was pretty and nice.

Stacey took hold of my arm and began to pull me along the hall. "Why don't we *happen* to pass by his locker?"

I pulled back. "This is dumb, Stacey."

"No it's not. Come on."

I let her drag me down the hall. Although I hadn't spent much time thinking about Pete, I'd always considered him a good guy. And cute. It might not be terrible to go to the dance with him.

The moment I saw him at his locker, though, I froze. I felt weird. Besides, I'd already told Dave I wasn't ready to go out with him. It wouldn't be fair or nice to then turn around and go to the dance with Pete.

I squirmed out of Stacey's grasp. But she grabbed my wrist.

"Hi, Pete!" Stacey called.

He looked at us and smiled.

We made some chitchat about school, then Stacey said, "So, are you guys psyched for the Fall Fling?"

"I guess," Pete said.

"Who are you going with, Mary Anne?" Stacey asked pointedly.

"No one," I replied. (Pete *had* to know what she was up to.)

"I have to go," Stacey said. "See you guys around."

Before we could say anything, she hurried away, leaving Pete and me alone together.

Pete watched Stacey leave, then he turned to me and smiled. "Do you get the feeling we've been set up?"

"Definitely," I replied.

"That's okay, though. Would you like to go to the Fall Fling with me?"

I just stood there. "Thank you, but . . ." I began. "You know I went out with Logan for so long . . . well . . . it seems like it's too soon to go out with someone new." That was true. I'd meant what I said to Dave. I wasn't ready for this.

"Okay," Pete replied.

"Thanks," I said again. "For asking . . . and for understanding."

He nodded.

I backed away a few steps, then turned and walked away quickly. My stomach growled and I realized I was hungry for lunch. But as I turned a corner in the hallway, I stopped short.

Logan stood in the hall, talking to Kristy.

And they were laughing.

Kristy even put her hand on his arm as she laughed.

What could they be saying to each other that was so funny? Why was she being all buddy-buddy with him?

Then a horrible thought hit me. What if Logan asked Kristy to the Fall Fling?

Would she accept?

The idea almost knocked the breath out of me.

I backed up out of their sight and leaned hard against the lockers, my mind racing.

There was no reason Kristy couldn't accept Logan's invitation. *I'd* broken up with *him*. It wasn't as if Logan had cut it off. I'd done the breaking up — so of course Kristy would think I didn't care who he dated.

Then why was the thought so terrible?

It just *was*.

How could I stand to see Logan and Kristy together? To hear her talk about him, about the things they did together?

I couldn't. But Kristy had been the one who stuck up for Logan when I told her I wanted to break it off. She liked him a lot. And he's always liked her.

But I never thought he liked her in *that* way.

"Wait a minute," I said to myself. "Get a grip." They were only talking. Maybe Kristy was just trying to cheer him up.

Still . . . I didn't like it.

Then an even more terrible thought came to me.

If Kristy and Logan became a couple, I'd probably lose Kristy as a best friend. And she was the only best friend I had left in Stoneybrook.

Suddenly I had a lot more sympathy for Claudia, who'd lost her best friend and the boy she liked too.

"You okay?"

I looked up and saw Dave Griffin looking at me with concern on his face. "Are you sick or something?"

"No, I'm fine," I replied, pushing away from the wall. My stomach chose that moment to growl loudly.

"Maybe you're a little hungry," Dave suggested with laughter in his eyes.

I had to laugh too. "I guess so."

"How about if I walk you to the lunchroom, to make sure you don't faint from hunger along the way?"

I smiled at this. "All right."

When we turned the corner, Logan and Kristy were gone. I wondered if they'd walked to the cafeteria together.

"Should I bother to ask you to the Fall Fling again?" he said.

"I'm not ready to go out," I replied. "But it's nice to be asked. Thank you."

"I don't get it, but okay," he said, still smiling. "I could understand if you just didn't want to go out with *me*, but why wouldn't you want to go at all?"

"I can't explain it."

"You're different from any girl I've ever met," he said.

"I think I'm pretty average."

"No. Other girls would be out looking for a new guy right away. But not you."

"Logan and I were very close," I told him. "You don't get over something like that so easily. And I disagree with what you said about other girls."

"Well, maybe it's not true. Anyway, I think you're unusual. In a good way."

"Thanks," I said.

I enjoyed talking to Dave. We stopped in front of the lunchroom and kept talking.

He told me a silly joke about a frog in a bank trying to get a loan. I burst out laughing.

It felt wonderful to laugh. I laughed so hard that tears came to my eyes.

And then I had the strong sense of someone staring at me. I looked up and found myself facing Logan.

He looked shocked.

Instantly, I stopped laughing.

And Logan whirled around, disappearing through the lunchroom doors.

❋ Chapter 10

On Friday I woke up with a slight headache and an uneasy stomach. "You should stay home," Sharon said, even though the thermometer showed a normal temperature. "You've been through a stressful time. You could probably use a rest."

I had no tests that day, so I agreed. "I feel a little guilty," I said as I climbed back into bed. "I could probably go."

"I don't want you getting sicker," she said. "I have to go to work, though. Will you be all right here alone?"

"Sure," I replied. Sharon brought me tea and toast and then left for work.

I went back to sleep. Soon I was dreaming that I was dressed in a wedding gown. Logan and I were walking up the aisle of a church together. All the while, Logan was talking to me. "I told you to wear a different gown," he said. I tore off the bottom quarter of the gown.

"Why did you have to put on so much make-up?" I used my veil to wipe the makeup from my face.

"Your heels are too high." I stopped and took off my shoes, tossing them over my shoulder.

"Those earrings are too bright," he continued.

"Stop!" I screamed at him. "Stop telling me what to do! Stop! Stop!" I began shaking.

Slowly, my eyes opened.

I was still shaking.

Only instead of Logan, I was looking at my father. "Mary Anne, wake up," he said, gently shaking me. "You're having a bad dream."

"Dad," I said, still half asleep. "What are you doing here?"

"I have an appointment downtown this afternoon," he explained, "so I figured I'd come home for lunch and see how you were doing. Sharon called me at the office to say you were home."

Dad's a lawyer and he often has appointments out of his office.

He smiled and tossed a rolled-up paper on my bed. "Good news," he told me. "The building inspector approved our plans this morning. We can go ahead and begin work on the new house."

"Really?" I cried, now fully awake.

Dad and Sharon had spent weeks working with an architect on plans to renovate the barn that's on the property where our old house had stood. Then they'd had to submit the plans to the town building department for approval.

I couldn't believe that eventually we'd be living in our barn, but Dad and Sharon had shown me the designs, and I had decided we were going to have one extremely cool house (and I don't mean drafty).

"I called the building contractors right away," he told me. "I'm going to meet them at the site tomorrow. Want to come? If you're feeling better, of course."

I frowned, thinking. There was a big football game the next day. It would mean seeing Logan, since he was on the team. Did I want to go to it?

Suddenly it seemed a lot easier to meet the contractors with Dad.

"I'll go," I told him.

He smiled at me. "How's your stomach? Want some lunch?"

I realized I was hungry. My headache was gone too. "Sure," I said, climbing out of bed.

On Saturday, at about ten, I walked toward Burnt Hill Road with Sharon and Dad. We passed kids going toward the game, some dressed in SMS jackets.

Dad and Sharon glanced at each other. "Sure you don't want to go to the game?" Sharon asked.

"There'll be others," I replied.

Dad squeezed my shoulder affectionately.

When we arrived at the burned-out place where our house had been, a man and woman were waiting there for us. "There are Ellice and Bob, our contractors," Dad told me.

"Hi," Ellice greeted us, smiling. "This place really smells like its name."

"It sure does," Sharon agreed.

I got it. *Burnt* Hill Road. Ha-ha.

"The first thing we'll have to do is bring in a Dumpster and a cleanup crew to haul away the debris," Bob said.

Good, I thought. *Get rid of all this old burned stuff. Start fresh.* The idea made me happy — which surprised me. Usually I like things to stay the way they are. And up until now all I'd felt when we talked about the new house was a sadness and long-ing for the old house. But here I was, eager for every-thing to be fresh and clean and brand-new.

It seemed I really was changing.

"When will it be ready to move into?" I asked.

Dad and Sharon looked to the contractors to an-swer that.

"Depends on the weather," Bob said. "If we don't have too much snow or rain, maybe by the new year."

I crossed my fingers and raised them to the sky, hoping the breezy but warm fall weather would con-tinue. I couldn't wait to move.

Dad and Sharon walked around the property with Bob, leaving me behind with Ellice. She was barely aware of me. She seemed to be concentrating on something.

Finally I said, "What are you thinking about?"

She jumped a little. "Oh, sorry," she said with a light laugh. "I'm also a landscaper. I did that before I got into contracting. I was imagining a garden."

"A garden?" I repeated.

"Your parents want me to do the landscaping once the house is finished. I was thinking about what plants would do best in this kind of soil and with this light. I think perhaps azalea bushes around the porch, maybe patches of daisies and wild heather toward the front, and a lamppost with hollyhocks wound around it." She pointed and gestured as she spoke, making it all seem so real.

I couldn't quite envision it because I wasn't sure what all the plants she had mentioned look like. It sounded beautiful, though.

"Is it hard to imagine a garden?" I asked.

"At first it was, but now it's easy. Once I learned about what could grow where, and with what kind of light, I just had to practice playing with the possibilities." She smiled at me. "It's sort of like life."

I must have appeared puzzled, because she explained, "In life, some choices are limited by circumstance. I probably couldn't be a sumo wrestler, for instance. And I'm already too old to start training as a ballet dancer. But there are a lot of opportunities still open to me. If I concentrate on those, the possibilities become nearly endless. The trick is not to box in your thinking."

"What do you mean?"

"Don't limit your thinking to what you already know. If I believe that only ferns and hostas will grow in low light, then that's all I'll ever plant in shade. On the other hand, if I explore other plants, and experiment, I might end up with some amazing results. If I thought of myself as only a landscaper, I wouldn't have started the contracting company with Bob."

Dad, Sharon, and Bob returned then. "Richard will come back to the office with us to work out the cleanup-crew details," Bob told Ellice, nodding to Dad.

"I'll head back with you," Sharon said to me. We said good-bye and began walking toward our rental house.

I couldn't stop thinking about what Ellice had said. It made so much sense. I'd kept myself in a box. I had thought of myself as shy, quiet Mary Anne, Logan's girlfriend. But now I'd taken myself out of that box. Even though it felt scary, maybe it was a good thing.

"You're quiet," Sharon noted as we walked. "What's on your mind?"

"Do you like change?" I asked her.

"I used to think I did," she replied. "Now I'm not as sure. Some changes in my life have been great, like marrying your dad. Others — Dawn and Jeff moving so far away, for instance — are not so good."

I nodded. "Lately, I want things to change."

"What things?" she asked.

"Our house," I said. "I wanted my relationship with Logan to change too. I guess that's why I broke it off."

Sharon smiled softly. "You're getting older," she said. "At your age, things have to change so you can see what the possibilities are."

Possibilities. There was that word again.

All that afternoon I wondered what my possibilities were.

❋ Chapter 11

On Sunday, Kristy phoned at about ten in the morning. "Mom and Watson are taking us apple and pumpkin picking. Want to come?"

I was still feeling a little weird about Kristy. Our Friday BSC meeting had been really strange. Claudia and Stacey still were not speaking to each other, and I wasn't saying much to Kristy. (I think everyone just assumed I wasn't feeling well since I'd been out of school that day.) There had been long, silent stretches of time. That almost never happens.

But I wanted everything to be okay between Kristy and me. And I love apple and pumpkin picking. "Sure," I replied.

I told my parents about Kristy's invitation, and Dad put in an order for Red Delicious apples. Sharon said whatever I brought home would be great. I dashed upstairs, dressed in jeans, a sweatshirt, and an orange fleece pullover, and was ready to go.

At about eleven o'clock a van arrived, driven by Watson, Kristy's stepfather. Kristy's two older brothers, Sam and Charlie, weren't there, but the younger members of her household — Karen, Andrew, David Michael, and Emily Michelle — were all belted in.

"Don't worry, this isn't a sitting job," Kristy said with a smile as I climbed in. "Mom and Watson are in charge."

I said hi to everyone and buckled up. Watson pulled out of the driveway, heading for the highway. "Why weren't you at the game yesterday?" Kristy asked me.

I didn't feel like discussing it in front of Kristy's family. "I wanted to see the contractors with my parents," I said instead. "We're about to start renovating the barn."

Watson and Kristy's mom had a million questions about the construction. Some I could answer, others not.

Their questions made the trip go quickly, and we were soon at the apple orchard, which was pretty crowded. Even though it wasn't a sitting job, Kristy and I helped watch the kids.

We stood in a line waiting for a hay wagon to

take us out to the apple trees. "Kristy told us you broke up with Logan," said Karen, who is seven.

"Yeah, she says you're crazy," added Andrew, who's four.

I looked sharply at Kristy.

"Andrew!" Kristy exclaimed.

"But that's what you said."

Kristy looked at me. "You know I didn't think you should do it," she explained.

"Thanks for calling me crazy," I muttered.

She rolled her eyes. "You weren't supposed to hear that."

The line suddenly moved forward, so I didn't have to answer her. A bunch of empty horse-drawn hay wagons pulled up, and we were able to fit our group onto one of them. By the time everyone was seated, Kristy was on one side, and I was on the other, with all the kids and Kristy's parents in between.

The ride through the orchard was bumpy but beautiful. The trees were heavy with apples of different kinds, some bright red, others green, and still others speckled with yellow. I could smell them from the wagon.

The wagon left us at a station where we bought bags to fill with apples. Watson put down a deposit for an apple picker, a long pole with tonglike grabbers that opened and closed. It would help snag apples too high up to reach by hand.

"This way, straight ahead," Kristy's mom said, studying a map of the orchard. "Let's start with the Macintosh apples over here, then we can move farther in for Granny Smiths. I want some Rome apples for pies too."

We headed into the orchard. In seconds, David Michael, who is seven, was up a tree, tossing apples down to Karen and Andrew.

Some branches were so heavy they dipped to the ground. Emily Michelle, Kristy's littlest sister, was able to pull fruit from those and fill her bag.

I found a tree and began picking. Kristy joined me. For a few minutes neither of us spoke. Finally Kristy turned to me. "Don't be mad," she said. "You know I understand why you and Logan broke up. But I do think Logan's a great guy."

Even though I was upset, I had to smile. I turned to pluck a low-growing apple so she wouldn't see my face.

"I know. It's just that our relationship was becoming boring." This was partly true.

"When you know someone a long time, things can't always be super-exciting," said Kristy, dropping an apple into her bag. "You get to know what he's going to do and say."

"It didn't feel right anymore."

"I guess you can't do anything about that," she admitted. "I'm sorry I called you crazy. I suppose I was feeling sorry for Logan when I said it."

We moved on to another tree. My bag was getting heavy already.

"Don't eat them all," I heard Kristy's mom warn the kids from a few trees over. "You'll get stomachaches."

"Karen is stuck in the tree!" Andrew cried.

"I'm coming," Watson called.

Kristy and I began picking side by side again. "How is Logan?" I asked.

"Not so great. But he'll survive."

"You would know."

Kristy turned to me. "What does that mean?"

"I saw you talking to him." I'd meant to say that very calmly. Instead, I said it fiercely, as if it were an accusation.

"So what? Now I'm not allowed to talk to him?"

"No!" I exclaimed. "I mean, you're supposed to be on my side."

"I can't believe you just said that! Why do I

have to take sides? Haven't you been wishing kids wouldn't do that?"

"Are you two going to the dance together?" The question just popped out of my mouth.

"What if we are?"

My jaw dropped. Was she admitting it? Tears sprang to my eyes. I turned so she wouldn't see them.

One tear spilled over. I ran off and ducked under another tree. I didn't know what else to do. I wasn't going to stand there in front of Kristy, crying.

I raised my hand to my eyes and let the tears soak the sleeve of my pullover.

How could Kristy go to the dance with Logan? How could she?

I couldn't care less if it didn't make sense, or if she had every right to date him. A real friend wouldn't. She'd care more about my feelings than about Logan.

After about five minutes, Karen found me. "Are you okay?" she asked.

"Just tired," I said.

"We're all going to the pumpkin patch now," she reported.

I lowered myself from the branch. "Thanks. I'm coming."

Kristy walked ahead with her parents and Emily Michelle. I hung back with David Michael, Karen, and Andrew. "Are you mad at Kristy?" Karen asked.

"A little," I admitted, trying to sound less upset than I felt.

She turned sharply to Andrew. "I told you. It's your fault for saying she was crazy."

"But Kristy said that," Andrew replied indignantly.

"It's okay," I told them. "Don't blame Andrew. He didn't realize."

"He realized," Karen muttered.

We continued walking until we came to a huge field filled with pumpkins. We laid our apple bags down in a pile. "Don't pick more pumpkins than you can carry," Watson warned us. "I'm not the pumpkin carrier."

We wandered into the pumpkin patch. Kristy and I headed in opposite directions. It was a peaceful place, despite all the people walking around. Everyone seemed wrapped up in his or her own thoughts as they tried to select the perfect pumpkin.

I thought more about Kristy and Logan. When I broke up with Logan, I knew he'd eventually go out with someone else. And what right did I have to say that Kristy couldn't be friends with Logan anymore? I still wanted to be friends with him myself.

I realized I had to tell her these things. I hadn't been fair to her. Then I felt a hand on my shoulder. Turning, I faced Kristy.

"I'm not going to the Fall Fling with Logan," she said. "He didn't ask me. And even if he had, I wouldn't have gone."

"It would be all right if you did," I replied. "I wouldn't like it, but I'd try to understand."

"I don't feel that way about Logan," said Kristy. "I just didn't want you telling me what to do or not do. It was silly. I'm sorry."

"I'm sorry too."

We smiled at each other and hugged. Then we sat down on two huge pumpkins growing side by side.

"Are you going to the dance with Dave Griffin?" Kristy asked me. "Logan thinks you are."

"No. I guess he saw us talking together and jumped to that conclusion."

"I know someone else who did something like that," she reminded me.

"You're right. Would you mind telling Logan I'm not going with Dave?"

"So now you want me to talk to him?"

"Sure. All you like."

"All right, then I'll tell him."

"You know," I said, "when I broke up with Logan, I thought it would be only between him and me. It seems, though, that it's affected everyone around us too."

I had to face the fact that I'd shaken up my entire world.

❋ Chapter 12

The next week went along a lot like the week before. Some kids still acted strange around me. Mostly it was Logan's friends who gave me dark looks.

Other kids, though, already seemed to be forgetting what had happened. The week before it had been a super-big deal. This week, most kids were talking about Cokie Mason, who was dating a new guy. I was old news.

Logan would say a quick hello to me anytime we met. Then he'd look away. It was hard even to catch his eye. I couldn't say two words to him before he would dash off.

That should have made things easier, or at least less complicated. But I had realized something. I missed talking to him. I wished we could still shoot ideas back and forth, laugh, and exchange opinions — as friends.

Stacey sighed when I told her Pete had asked me to the dance but I'd said no. "You're hopeless," she commented. "You're staying loyal to a boy you've already broken up with. It makes no sense."

"I know."

She sighed again. "Tell me you're at least going to the dance, even if you don't go with someone."

"I don't think so."

"But you might dance with someone new and something might come from that."

"If I wanted to be with someone new, I'd have said I'd go with Dave or Pete."

"I give up!" Stacey cried. "Do what you want."

Hearing her say that made me realize that I *was* doing what I wanted. Neither Logan nor my friends were taking the lead.

I was. And feeling pretty proud of it.

No, I wasn't going to let anyone pressure me into going to the dance.

I felt great about that decision and my newfound independence — until Saturday afternoon.

Then, suddenly, instead of feeling strong and in control, I felt lonely. I sat on the living room couch and wondered what was wrong with me. Why hadn't

I wanted to go to the dance? Was everyone at SMS going except me?

Was Logan going?

I had no idea. At Friday's BSC meeting, we'd avoided the subject. Between my state and the whole Claudia-Jeremy-Stacey thing, it was just too uncomfortable.

I found the cordless phone and called Claudia. "Are you going to the dance?" I asked.

"No. There's no way I want to be anywhere near Stacey and Jeremy when they're dancing together. That's one experience I can live without."

Great, I thought as I wandered back into the living room and stretched out on the couch. *At least I won't have to be alone.* "Want to come over and hang out at my house?"

"Sorry. I can't. I'm sitting for the Rodowskys tonight. Try Kristy. I know she's not going."

"Okay. 'Bye."

Before I could punch in Kristy's number, Dad entered the living room. "Sharon and I are going to the movies tonight. Want to join us?" he asked.

"No thanks," I replied. My parents are great, but I didn't feel like going out with them. "I'll do something with one of my friends."

"Well . . . all right." He left me to call Kristy.

"Hi," said Kristy when she picked up the phone. "I can't talk long. I'm helping Nannie make a zillion apple pies." Nannie is Kristy's grandmother.

"Why are you making so many?" I asked.

"We're donating them to the homeless shelter. We could never eat all these apples in a million years. We're making pumpkin pies too."

"Well, when you're done, would you like to come over? Dad and Sharon are going out. We could nuke some popcorn and watch videos."

"It sounds great, but I have to go to a chamber of commerce dinner tonight. They're honoring Watson."

"Oh," I said glumly.

"Go to the dance by yourself."

"I'm not going if you guys aren't," I said. "I don't want to hang out by myself."

"I'm sorry, Mary Anne. Really I am. I'll call you tomorrow. Maybe we can do something then."

"All right. Have fun at the dinner. 'Bye." I hung up, sighing.

Deal with it, Mary Anne, I commanded myself. I'd wanted to be on my own. Now I was getting what I'd asked for.

That evening, after supper, Dad and Sharon

again invited me to go out with them. I was tempted, but resisted.

"Are you sure you'll be all right tonight?" Dad asked.

"Dad!" I cried.

"Okay. Okay," he said. "I just don't want you here alone thinking about the dance and all."

"I'll be fine," I insisted.

After I locked the door behind them, I went to the kitchen and put a bag of popcorn into the microwave. While it cooked, I opened the living room cabinet where we keep the videos. We have a pretty big collection.

I began pulling out my favorites. I'd selected three when the microwave beeped, signaling me that the popcorn was done. I dumped my selections on the couch and returned to the kitchen.

Popcorn in hand, I sat on the couch and looked through the videos, deciding which one to watch first.

I picked up *Fly Away Home*, about a girl who raises baby geese and teaches them to fly, using a hang glider. I remembered watching it with Logan. There's this really touching moment when the baby geese first fly. Naturally, I was blubbering my eyes out. (I not only cry at sad parts of movies, I also cry at happy parts.) I had looked over at Logan and seen that his eyes were misty. At that moment, I felt so in love with him. Any boy who could get weepy over flying baby geese had to be the greatest, most sensitive guy on earth.

Hmm. With all those memories attached, it probably wasn't the best movie for me to watch just then.

I set it aside.

The next one was *When Harry Met Sally*, about two people who keep falling in and out of love.

Not exactly what I wanted to watch right now.

My third choice was a movie about a talking parrot. *Paulie*. Logan and I had argued over that one. I'd thought it was sweet. He'd said it was dumb. It had bothered me that he wouldn't let it go until he had changed my mind about it. That night I'd given in and said, "Okay, I suppose it was dumb, but I still liked it."

For the rest of that evening I'd been annoyed at myself for giving in. I suppose that by then, things were already beginning to change between Logan and me, only I hadn't realized it yet.

I put that one aside also. I knew I'd only be aggravated as I watched it.

I was about to search for another video when the

phone rang. I hurried to the kitchen and grabbed the receiver, hoping Claudia or Kristy had somehow become free for the evening.

"It's me. . . ." said the voice on the other end.

Logan.

"Hi," I said shakily. He was the last person I'd expected.

"I guess you didn't go to the dance," he said after a moment.

"Nope," I replied. "You either."

"No. I didn't want to. What are you doing?"

"Deciding what video to watch."

"Are Kristy and the others with you?"

"No. I'm alone tonight."

"Me too."

More silence.

"What did you decide to watch?" he asked.

"I haven't picked one yet." I wasn't about to tell him that he was the problem — that I was desperately searching for a movie that didn't remind me of him.

"I rented the Robin Williams movie, the one that just came out on video," he said. "Want to see it?"

My brain felt scrambled. I wasn't sure how to answer. I was happy that Logan was being friendly. And I really didn't want to be in some weird war with him. But I didn't want to give him the wrong idea — that I was open to the idea of getting back together.

"Thanks," I said. "I'll get it from you at school on Monday."

"Or," he said, "I could bring it over to you tonight."

"Don't you want to see it first?" I asked.

"We could watch it together."

I didn't answer.

"As friends, I mean," he added quickly. "You said that's what you wanted. And . . . I guess I'm willing to try. It's better than nothing."

"Okay," I agreed. "Come on over." The truth was, I did want to see him.

After I hung up, I stood there wondering if I'd done the right thing. Feeling panicked, I phoned Claudia at the Rodowskys'.

"I might have just done a stupid thing," I told her when she picked up. "I invited Logan over."

"Will your parents mind?" she asked.

"No. But what if he gets the wrong idea?"

"Make it clear right from the start," she advised. "Keep things very unromantic. Don't sit too close to him." In the background I heard a crash. "I think

Jackie just broke something," she said. "I better go. Good luck."

"Thanks," I said.

As I hung up the phone, the front doorbell rang. I froze, staring at the door.

❋ Chapter 13

"How did you get here so fast?" I asked as I opened the door to Logan.

"Dad dropped me off," he answered, stepping inside. "He was going out anyway."

He looked around the living room and squinted. "Why do you have so many lights on?" he asked.

I hadn't expected him to notice. I'd turned on almost all the lights in the kitchen and the living room, to make the place as unromantic as I could.

"Oh, you're right," I said. "Look at that." I snapped off a couple of lamps but still left the place pretty bright.

He held out the video and a big bag of potato chips. "Want some soda?" I offered.

"Sure," he agreed, and followed me into the kitchen.

I felt a little jittery, but mostly I was happy. It was good to see Logan without a lot of people staring at us.

As I poured the soda, Logan began talking about that afternoon's football game. I already knew we'd won, but he told me about a play that had gone wrong yet resulted in a touchdown anyway.

I laughed when he said how he'd been totally confused but kept running with the ball because he couldn't find anyone to pass it to.

"You made the touchdown?" I asked.

"Yeah, it was total dumb luck. I was like . . . duh . . . how did this happen?"

We laughed.

Everything began to feel normal.

We returned to the living room and popped in the video. While we watched the previews, I told him about the plans for the new house. "My room will be a lot bigger than the old one was. Even though I loved it, our old house *was* old and dark. The barn is going to be sunny and open. I can't wait."

"Sounds great," he said. "You'll have to invite me over to see it when it's done."

"Definitely. Maybe I'll even ask if I can have a party."

The feature presentation came on and we quieted

down. One thing Logan and I have always agreed on is Robin Williams. We both think that when he's funny, there's no one funnier. (We disagree about him when he's serious. I think he's sweet. Logan can't stand him in those roles.)

In this movie he was hysterical. By the middle of it, we were both howling with laughter.

"See?" Logan said to me, still a little breathless from laughing. "We still have fun together."

"You're right," I agreed, smiling. "We do."

His expression turned serious. "Then I don't understand why we have to be apart."

My smile faded quickly.

"Really," he continued. "As long as we still like each other and have fun, why can't we work out our other problems?"

I drew in a long, slow breath, no longer paying attention to the movie. "We've tried to work out the problems before," I reminded him as calmly as I could.

"Mary Anne, don't get excited about what I'm going to say, okay?"

"I'll try not to."

"You've been through a lot lately," he began. "I've been wondering if . . . if maybe the fire upset you so much that you're not thinking clearly."

"Are you kidding? Are you saying that I'm acting crazy?"

"Not crazy," he said quickly. "Just . . . not like yourself. It's as if you're kind of off balance."

What was he trying to say? That because I no longer wanted to go out with him, I must be out of my mind?

"Maybe I want to be off balance," I replied. "Maybe I was tired of being balanced the way you wanted me to be."

"You are so wrong about me," Logan exclaimed. "I do not push you around or make you do things my way. I've been thinking about it and it's not true. That's just the way you see things."

"How can I see things differently from the way I see them?" I snapped. "That's the stupidest thing I've ever heard!"

"Don't call me stupid!"

"You're not stupid, but what you just said was stupid. It proves my point, though. You don't even want me to trust my own judgment."

"I do so!"

"No. You don't. Did you hear what you said? 'It's just the way you see things.' You want me to see things your way."

"You think about things too much," Logan

said, standing up and walking toward the window.

"How can a person think too much?"

"I don't know. But you do," he insisted, gazing out the window. Then he turned abruptly, facing me once again. "Let's make it simple. So I can understand," he said. "What is it exactly that you no longer like about me?"

"You're too possessive," I answered.

"Well, you're too sensitive."

"Maybe, but you're not sensitive at all." That wasn't entirely true, I realized. "At least you're not sensitive to me and my feelings."

"You expect me to be a mind reader," Logan said fiercely. "No one will ever be able to make you happy, because you expect everyone to be as sensitive as you are. No guy on earth could be that much in tune with your every feeling."

I glared at him. This was so unfair.

"Maybe someday they'll explore another planet and find some alien race of mind readers," he went on. "Then you'll find the guy you're looking for."

"Very funny," I replied. "I think it's time for you to go home." I stalked over to the VCR and stopped the tape. I dropped it back into its case and handed it to him.

Logan took it, then sat on the couch.

He didn't seem to be leaving, so I retrieved his jacket from the front hall and gave it to him.

"I didn't mean to make you mad," he said.

"It's a little late to worry about that now."

"Sorry."

That quick apology slowed down my anger. "It's okay," I muttered.

"Mary Anne, I just think that even after everything that's happened, we can still save our relationship," he said.

I thought about that. I thought hard. Was he right? And . . . was that what I wanted?

I still had so many strong feelings for him. It had felt so right, laughing with him. And it would be so nice not to feel lonely and anxious. It was all so confusing. A dull ache began throbbing in my temples.

Logan stood and headed for the door. "I'll leave if it's what you really want," he said.

This was my chance to take it all back, my moment to turn back time and set everything right again. But I couldn't.

I knew I'd already done the best thing for myself. I needed to be free of Logan. Deep inside I was sure some part of me would never get the chance to be born — to grow — if I lost my nerve now. I remembered Ellice and her words about possibilities. I *wanted* my possibilities. With Logan choking them off I'd never know what they might have been.

"It's the best thing," I answered in a dry, cracked voice.

He opened the door but hesitated. "You're wrong about that."

"I don't think so," I replied quietly.

Then he was gone.

And I couldn't stop the tears from streaming down my face.

❀ Chapter 14

"Mary Anne, calm down. You're getting hysterical. Take a deep breath," said Dawn. I'd called her about five minutes after Logan left.

Holding the phone away from my face, I tried to do as she said and calm myself.

My sleeve was now soaked from wiping away tears. I walked to the kitchen for a paper towel and blotted my eyes, then blew my nose.

I breathed in deeply and slowly. But then I began to hiccup. "Oh, great," I muttered into the phone, hiccuping in between words.

Dawn laughed. "Oh, no, hiccups. Get some water. You sip. I'll talk."

"O-*hic*-kay," I agreed, taking a cup from a kitchen cupboard.

"It might seem like the end of the world now,"

said Dawn. "You've done the right thing, though. Ever since I've known you you've defined yourself by your relationship to someone."

"What do you mean?" I asked.

"When we met, you were your dad's little girl. You dressed the way he wanted you to and obeyed all his rules."

"It wasn't as if I had much choice about it."

"That's true. Still, you didn't seem to mind all that much."

"I minded," I argued.

"The other thing you were when I met you was a BSC member," Dawn continued. "The first thing you did was get me to join."

"You make it sound as if there's something wrong with that." (My hiccups had disappeared.)

"There isn't. It's great to be part of a group, but you have to know who you are outside the group."

"I may not be as much of an individual as you are," I said. "But I know who I am . . . I think."

"Then you became Logan's girlfriend," Dawn continued. "There you were — a BSC member and Logan's girlfriend."

"I don't understand your point," I said. "What am I supposed to do? Go around like some lone wolf, not connecting to anything or anyone?"

"Of course not!" she cried. "Listen. I love you, Mary Anne. I'm not trying to hurt your feelings. What I'm asking is — who would you be if you didn't have the BSC and Logan?"

"I'd still be me."

"Right. But who *are* you? What do you like to do? Most of your time has been divided between BSC activities and Logan."

To my surprise, I began crying again.

"I'm sorry! I'm sorry!" she said frantically. "I didn't want to make you cry. Forget I said anything. I don't even know what I'm talking about."

"It's not you," I sobbed. "It's me. You're right. I'm not sure who I am without my friends, especially Logan. Dawn, I don't want to be all alone!"

"No one does. But you'll never be alone, Mary Anne. You have our parents. And me. I know I'm far away, but there's always the phone. All our friends in Stoneybrook love you too. Especially Kristy. She's been your best friend since you were little."

"But what if . . . what if . . . what if I change so much I lose all that?"

"That's not going to happen. You won't change into anything terrible. You'll only become more Mary Anne. More yourself. I know it."

"I don't know it," I said.

"Believe me, it's true. I've seen it coming for awhile now. You're busting loose, Mary Anne."

That made me laugh a little. Me — quiet, sensitive Mary Anne — busting loose?

Only Dawn would see it that way.

"We better hang up," I said. "This is costing a fortune."

"All right. I'll call you tomorrow."

"Thanks," I said. " 'Bye."

After hanging up, I sat a minute and let my tears dry. Then I went to the closet for my jacket. Opening the front door, I stepped outside.

As I'd hoped, the chilly October air made me feel better. Jamming my hands into my pockets, I began walking down the street. Our neighbors had begun putting up Halloween decorations. A few jack-o'-lanterns grinned at me from doorsteps. Scarecrows flapped in the night breeze.

When I was small, I lived on this block with Dad. Kristy had been my next-door neighbor. Then she moved across town with her mom and brothers to Watson's mansion. And eventually I moved to Sharon's house, when she and Dad married.

But now I was back — across the street from my old house.

Was it the closing of a full circle?

I suppose you can never really know about things like that.

Memories crowded into my head. I remembered being little and running around the neighborhood. It seemed long ago, although it really wasn't so many years in the past.

I kept walking until I reached the Rodowskys' house. I turned up the walk and rang the bell.

"Mary Anne?" Claudia said when she answered. "Wow! You look all . . . puffy. You've been crying. Come in."

Taking hold of my arm, she drew me inside. "The boys are already in bed. Jackie and Archie are asleep. Shea's reading. Are you okay?"

I took off my jacket and told her what had happened between Logan and me. Then I filled her in on what Dawn had said.

"Dawn goes a little overboard sometimes," Claudia suggested gently.

I smiled at that. "The only person I know who is more of an individual than Dawn is you, Claudia."

"Thanks . . . I guess," she said, sitting on the couch next to me. "Do you want to be more of an individual?"

"I want to be who I really am," I said, speaking slowly, struggling to choose exactly the right words to express what I meant. "Maybe I mush myself around too much to make people happy."

"It's possible," Claudia said, watching me closely.

"Is that what you really think?" I asked her. "That I make myself into whatever people around me want me to be?"

"Sometimes. That's sort of nice for the people around you. I'm sure my parents wish I were more agreeable. It might not be the best thing for you, though. Besides, you can't please everyone."

"I wonder if I've been trying to please too many people," I said. Was that why I was feeling so unsettled? Had I been pulling myself in too many directions?

I would have to think about it.

Chapter 15

On Sunday morning, I woke up feeling better than I had since I broke up with Logan. I wasn't sure why. I sat up in bed and hugged my knees. What had happened to make me feel so good?

Was it something Dawn or Claudia had said? Or maybe it was simply the fact that they'd been there. It made me less fearful about being alone again in the future.

Maybe the fight with Logan had finally cleared the air. Somehow our relationship now seemed officially over. Was I relieved about that?

Possibly.

Probably.

My bedroom door creaked slightly. I turned in time to see Stacey, Claudia, and Kristy burst into my room. Kristy bounced onto the bed. "Wake up!" she cried, grabbing my pillow and batting me over the head with it.

"Hey, cut it out!" I yelped, laughing.

Stacey and Claudia went to opposite sides of my bed. "Just what you need on a Sunday morning," Stacey said with a laugh. "Us!"

I glanced at my clock. It was almost ten. Not exactly the crack of dawn. Still, my friends don't usually pounce on me on Sunday mornings. "What are you guys doing here?"

"We met up on our way over to visit you," Claudia explained.

"You mean you didn't plan this?" I said.

"Nope," Kristy replied.

"Wow. Thanks. I'm feeling a lot better. You three are the best friends." I meant it too. Imagine! Each of them was so concerned that she was on her way to check on me. Even Stacey and Claudia seemed to have struck some kind of truce, at least for the day. I couldn't ask for better friends than that.

"How was the dance?" I asked Stacey.

"Good. Dave Griffin kept trying to talk to me about you. He was there by himself. Pete Black came with Grace Blume. They're not a good match. I bet you could still have a chance with him if you wanted."

"I don't even want to think about boys or dating or anything like that for awhile," I told her.

"What do you want to do?" Kristy asked. "It's a great day."

"There are a bunch of outdoor craft fairs in Stamford," I recalled. "I could ask my dad to drive us somewhere."

"Good idea! I love craft fairs," Claudia said. "Hand-painted shirts! Art!"

"Great food," Kristy added.

"I love craft-fair jewelry," Stacey put in. I could tell it took some effort for her to agree with Claudia.

"Let's go!" I said, jumping out of bed. I pulled on a long-sleeved T-shirt, overalls, sneakers, and a heavy sweater. "Dad!" I called as I led the others down the stairs.

No one answered.

"Where'd they go?" I asked, checking around the house.

"There's a note on your kitchen table," Kristy announced. "It says, 'Gone to barn. Be back soon.' "

"Want to go over there and find them?" I asked.

"Okay," said my friends.

Together we headed for Burnt Hill Road. On the way I told them more about the plans for our new home.

When we reached our street I spotted a long, wide Dumpster sitting in front of the place where our house once stood. We hurried to the barn and saw Dad and Sharon standing in front of it.

"Hi," Dad greeted me and my friends. "Say good-bye to the last, ashy remains of our things. It's all getting hauled away."

Ellice handed Sharon a twisted piece of sooty metal. "This looked to me like real silver," she said.

Sharon examined the bent shape. "I know what this is," she said, looking sadly at Dad. "It's the frame of our wedding picture."

He put his arm around her and squeezed. "Our friends will send us the pictures they have," he said. "We'll buy an even better frame."

She smiled softly at him.

"All the best things are still ahead of us," he added. "I'm looking forward to starting over — everything fresh and new."

I understood how he felt. Not everyone gets a chance for a fresh start.

I asked Dad and Sharon if they could take us into Stamford. "Give us ten minutes and we'll go with you," Dad agreed.

My friends and I walked into our yard. Wordlessly we stared at the barn. "I can't picture it as a house," Stacey said.

"I can," I said. I could too. My new home shimmered there in the sunlight for me.

Then, in my mind, I saw something unexpected.

An imaginary girl was walking out the front door of my imaginary house. She was petite, with bouncy brown hair and big brown eyes. There was energy in her steps. Her smile shone.

And suddenly I recognized her. She was me. A little older, fifteen maybe. The new Mary Anne of the future, stepping out of her new house. This girl was confident, ready for whatever the day held.

"What are you staring at?" Kristy asked me.

"Oh, nothing," I said with a smile.

She'd have thought I was crazy if I told her.

"It's really a great day, isn't it?" I said to my friends.

They nodded, smiling.

"I think you're going to be all right, Mary Anne," Stacey said warmly. "Even without Logan."

"You're right," I agreed. "It helps to have great friends."

I looked back at the house. Mary Anne of the

future gazed at me happily. She wasn't MaryAnne-andLogan. Or MaryAnneandtheBSC.

She was MaryAnneherownself.

I couldn't wait for the day when I'd get to know her better.

Ann M. Martin

About the Author

ANN MATTHEWS MARTIN was born on August 12, 1955. She grew up in Princeton, NJ, with her parents and her younger sister, Jane.

Although Ann used to be a teacher and then an editor of children's books, she's now a full-time writer. She gets ideas for her books from many different places. Some are based on personal experiences. Others are based on childhood memories and feelings. Many are written about contemporary problems or events.

All of Ann's characters, even the members of the Baby-sitters Club, are made up. (So is Stoneybrook.) But many of her characters are based on real people. Sometimes Ann names her characters after people she knows; other times she chooses names she likes.

In addition to the Baby-sitters Club books, Ann Martin has written many other books for children. Her favorite is *Ten Kids, No Pets* because she loves big families and she loves animals. Her favorite BSC book is *Kristy's Big Day.* (Kristy is her favorite baby-sitter.)

Ann M. Martin now lives in New York with her cats, Gussie, Woody, and Willy, and her dog, Sadie. Her hobbies are reading, sewing, and needlework — especially making clothes for children.

Look for #4

CLAUDIA AND THE FRIENDSHIP FEUD

Jeremy and I talked about everything *except* Stacey.

I looked over at the clock. Nine twenty-one P.M.

We'd been on the phone for almost an hour.

"Do you realize that it's almost nine-thirty?" I said.

"No way!" he said. "I'll be in trouble if my dad finds out I'm still on the phone. It's so late and it's Sunday! Won't your parents get mad?"

"Well, I have my own phone."

Jeremy sounded impressed. "Wow."

I wasn't about to explain the BSC to him then, so I left it at that.

"So I guess I'll see you around school," Jeremy joked.

"Around every corner, apparently," I said.

"I'm glad we talked, Claudia."

"Me too. Have a good night."

As I hung up the phone, I heard it again — loud thumping inside my chest. And my mind was racing.

If Stacey knew what had just happened she would —

Better not to think about it.

Stacey didn't have anything to do with Jeremy's calling me. It was his decision and his decision alone. Besides, he just wanted a friend. He was NOT flirting. He was just talking. Jeremy Rudolph was still dating Stacey McGill. He'd said that.

I reached into my closet to sneak one of the cookies from my secret stash. It was time to eat something sweet.

I, Claudia Kishi, eat whenever I am stressed. And *really*, really confused — like right now.

I wondered if Jeremy felt the same way.

Baby-sitters Club

Friends BSC Forever

Check out what's new with your old friends.